MOMologues 2: Off to School

by Lisa Rafferty, Stefanie Cloutier and Sheila Eppolito

Contributing Writer: Charlotte Dietz

A SAMUEL FRENCH ACTING EDITION

SAMUEL FRENCH

FOUNDED 1830

SAMUELFRENCH.COM

ISBN 978-0-573-70027-9   Printed in U.S.A.   #20268

MUSIC USE NOTE

Licensees are solely responsible for obtaining formal written permission from copyright owners to use copyrighted music in the performance of this play and are strongly cautioned to do so. If no such permission is obtained by the licensee, then the licensee must use only original music that the licensee owns and controls. Licensees are solely responsible and liable for all music clearances and shall indemnify the copyright owners of the play and their licensing agent, Samuel French, Inc., against any costs, expenses, losses and liabilities arising from the use of music by licensees.

IMPORTANT BILLING AND CREDIT
REQUIREMENTS

All producers of *MOMologues 2: Off to School must* give credit to the Authors of the Play in all programs distributed in connection with performances of the Play, and in all instances in which the title of the Play appears for the purposes of advertising, publicizing or otherwise exploiting the Play and/or a production. The names of the Authors *must* appear on a separate line on which no other name appears, immediately following the title and *must* appear in size of type not less than fifty percent of the size of the title type.

In addition the following credit *must* be given in all programs and publicity information distributed in association with this piece:

MOMologues 2: Off To School
By Lisa Rafferty, Stefanie Cloutier and Sheila Eppolito
Contributing Writer: Charlotte Dietz

MOMologues 2: Off to School premiered at the Regent Theatre in Arlington, Massachusetts on Thursday, May 12, 2005. It was directed by Lisa Rafferty and stage managed by Kristie Froman, with lighting design by Francesca Bastianini and set design by Derek Till. The original cast was Stefanie Cloutier, Charlotte Dietz, Cinda Donovan, and Maria Wardwell.

The show was subsequently presented at the Palace Theatre in Manchester, New Hampshire, and the Company Theatre in Norwell, Massachusetts. It returned to the Regent Theatre in September 2005.

CHARACTERS

LYNETTE
TRICIA
LEA
CAROLINE

(As cast walks onstage, and lights come up, we hear the Stone's "19th Nervous Breakdown.")*

LYN. *(Music continues to underscore the following.)* Someone told me there would be a lot of crying during the first five years. I had no idea it would be me doing most of it...

LEA. Homework, soccer practice, dance recitals, medical forms, cub scouts, Family Fun Night, doctor's visits, playdates, car pools... A mom's life...

TRICIA. Full time mother, full time career, full time wife, full time daughter. Full-time medication *(shakes Rx bottle)* is the only way to get me though it all...

CAR. Willful disobedience. That's what puts me over the edge. Being naughty because my son is tired or hungry, or being naughty because my daughter is growing up or going through a phase or had a bad day at school. But it's the WILLFUL disobedience that gets me. The "up yours Mom" attitude. The "I know I'm being bad, I'm doing it ON PURPOSE." Yup. That's what will really put me in the padded room...

(Music fades out by the end of CAROLINE's monologue. All exit except TRICIA.)

(TRICIA sits, pulls books out of briefcase.)

TRICIA. It all started when I got pregnant the first time, and someone gave me "What to Expect When You're Expecting." Since I'd never BEEN pregnant before, I felt relieved to have this expert advice right at my fingertips. Then, at the baby shower, someone gave me "What to Expect the First Year" and I felt good. I kept checking the baby's progress, making sure the baby was "up to code," so to speak. Then came

---

* Please see Music Use Note on Page 3.

"What to Expect the Toddler Years," and I also picked up Brazelton's "Touchpoints" and Penelope Leach's "Your Baby and Child." But it didn't stop there. After I had another kid, and the kids got older, and the issues more complex, I began stalking the parenting section of the bookstore... Nothing will make you feel more inadequate than shelves of parenting books. How could I have missed "The Mighty Toddler: The Essential Guide to the Toddler Years"? Or "Proactive Parenting: Guiding Your Child from Two to Six"? What if they had incredibly important information I needed? If you have girls, you HAVE to read "Reviving Ophelia," and obviously "Raising Cain" will help you with boys. Then, of course, my children developed disturbing behaviors, so I found myself flipping through "The Explosive Child" and "The Out-of Sync Child," and "Raising Your Spirited Child." Now I know I'm screwing up my kids in more ways than I thought possible... Is this INSANE or what? Can someone please stop me? Is there a book I could read to help with this madness? (**TRICIA** *exits to go look for another book...*)

(**LEA** *enters holding bag and car keys.*)

LEA. So it's Sunday morning and my husband is out of town so it's up to me to get the three kids ready for the 9:00 o'clock mass. I had rejected bathing suits and nudity as possible church outfits, packed baggies of crayons and coloring books, grabbed the church donation envelope and a bottle for the baby. We all pile into the car and its 8:58. Gotta fly! So I clear the garage and floor it – forgetting that my husband's car is behind me. Smash...Fuuuucck.... Now I DEFINITELY have to go to church...So we make it there and we're sitting toward the front as I congratulate myself. Look at me – husband out of town, car accident, 3 kids and I still made it to church. Then my middle one whispers to me "is that Him?" I look around expecting a neighbor or something. "Is that Him?" she asks again. "Is that the Yucky Jesus?" she asks, pointing at the cross.

"Shh, no honey," I whisper, "Jesus isn't yucky. Because of Him, we can make mistakes and still go to heaven." "NO!" I know it's the Yucky Jesus. I went to Emma's birthday party there." And then I get it. Yucky Jesus. Chuck E. Cheese's…. One in the same. God help me. *(She exits.)*

(CAROLINE and LYNETTE enter a coffee shop.)

LYN. Okay, I've got my coffee, and I've got 10 minutes.

CAR. Well, I'll get right to the big news…My youngest is FINALLY potty-trained.

LYN. whoo-hoo…

CAR. Yes, bribery…The M&M's trick – 1 for number 1 and 2 for…you know the drill…but it was worth it: he's finally kicked the diaper habit. Three kids, 7 years later, a landfill of Huggies and I'm done with diapers.

LYN. Yeah, there's nothing like what I like to call my "incentive-based program…" We've been talking about that at my parenting group…

CAR. Please tell me you're not in ANOTHER one? What's the name of this one, "How to yell so kids won't talk back?"

LYN. No, that was the eight-week course I took. This one is an ongoing group on how to cope with raising siblings.

CAR. You mean there's a group for that?! And here I've just been trying to slog through it on my own…

LYN. Hey – I like it…Lets me talk to other moms about the things that drive us crazy. You know, kids beating the crap out of each other, the teasing, the fighting, fighting, fighting…How insane you feel by the end of the day.

CAR. Wow, who knew? So what is this, your fourth parenting group?

LYN. Listen, some of us just don't have that knack for motherhood, ya know?… I feel so overwhelmed, and who has time to read books? I'd rather just take a quick course and have someone else give me the highlights, like Cliff Notes for parents.

CAR. Has it worked?

LYN. Well, I started with "Understanding your Toddler" and "Positive Discipline" – talk about an oxymoron – then I checked out "Birds, Bees and Beyond" so I know how to answer the big sex talk...

CAR. So?

LYN. It still hasn't come up...And now I've forgotten everything they taught me...

CAR. Didn't you take notes?

LYN. Of course I did, but they're all mixed in with the seminar I took on emotional intelligence, and the one on how to handle your anger...

CAR. Ok, you are really scaring me now...C'mon on – how ARE you supposed to deal with anger?

LYN. Actually, I had PMS and was too pissed off that night to take any real notes. But it was a great venting session.

CAR. I can't find time to pee by myself; where do you find the time for all these parenting classes?

LYN. I convince my husband I need the ongoing education to be the best mother I can be. Plus, it's a night out.

CAR. I hear that...

LYN. Anyway, I just signed up for a new class...

CAR. WHAT?

LYN. Only THIS one is over the internet, so all I have to do is log on after the kids are asleep, and participate in the online discussion.

CAR. Cut it out...what's it called?

LYN. "Parenting the Strong-Willed Child."

CAR. C'mon do you think it will help?

LYN. Probably not, but I gotta keep hoping...

CAR. Yeah, well email me those highlights, okay?

(They exit.)

(LEA enters.)

LEA. Okay, what is up with playdates? Kind of sounds like the times you went out with a guy you didn't really like, just for practice. Which is kind of what it is…There were no playdates when I was a kid. I got sent outside to play, and I ran around the neighborhood, knocking on doors, until someone came out. And I played until dark, or until my mom called me back home. Did she have any idea where I was? Did she know I was building cardboard forts and bringing lighted candles inside? Did she know we were climbing pine trees taller than buildings? Nooooo… So, now we have playdates, totally civilized things where one mom calls another to arrange a time for two children to play together. With snacks and everything. Maybe even a designated activity, like rollerblading, or bead stringing… At first, I got to pick the kids my kids had these playdates with: I knew the moms, we'd get a chance to gab while the kids played. But now that they're older, my kids insist on picking their own playdates. Which means I don't always know the moms, or even the kids, for that matter. But I get on the phone, introduce myself, invite the other child, detail the activity so everyone feels comfortable. I know the day is coming when they will make their own phone calls, devise their own plans. And that this is all just a precursor to real dating, with kids of the opposite sex or whatever – who knows? And movies, experimental kissing and hooking up… You know, I think I'll just go make a few phone calls, see if I can set up something for Tuesday… *(She exits.)*

(TRICIA enters – at the kitchen counter:)

TRICIA. Okay, true confessions….. You have a kid over for a play date. You notice he's got gross, greenish Howard Hughes fingernails. Do you immediately judge the mother? I do! I know it's not fair, but I can't help it. Or when you read about some crazy murderer, do you wonder about the mom? Like Jeffrey Dahmer and Charles Manson…were their moms good nail-clipping moms who whipped up Toll House cookies? My daughter had a friend over, and he snapped the heads off eight Barbies. Eight! Now I don't like Barbie that much, but to see her beheaded with abandon is a little unsettling. Is this how it starts? Barbie heads today, human parts in the freezer tomorrow? I know it's ridiculous, thinking there's a slippery slope from unflossed teeth to mass murder... The big "nature versus nurture" controversy. The sick truth is, I have to believe that the nurture part matters lots, or how else do I get excited about flossing, laundry, sunscreen? If the kids are totally predetermined to be who and what they're going to be without me, then why bother? I'm killing myself to make them kind, clean, funny, and open hearted. What if, at the end of the line, I've raised a bunch of mean, dirty, dull, small-minded wretches?... See, it's all about the mother. If a child is perfectly coifed and well behaved, I look at the mom admiringly from every angle, searching for clues. Same goes for bad manners, crusty noses, little self-important kids, kids with their hands in their pants. We didn't sign up for this when we wanted to have children! But if you drop the ball on any of it, you're the crappy mom. And if there IS anything to the nurture thing, I'd better do it well. So I dutifully fill out those permission slips, wipe a nose, pick out a good outfit for picture day, volunteer in the classroom, and wear some makeup. Be the fun sleepover mom, decorate those holiday cookies, and match up those socks. It all better be important. *(She exits.)*

(Enter **CAROLINE,** **LEA,** *and* **LYNETTE,** *Aretha Franklin's Think (Freedom)* * underscores as they ad lib goodbyes to kids getting on the bus ["see you after school, honey! Have a good day!" "I'll dismiss you later" or whatever...].)*

LEA. Whoo hoo! Thought they'd never get on that bus...

---

* Please see Music Use Note on Page 3.

LYN. It was touch and go all morning, I just barely held it together until they were out the door with backpacks on...

(The chorus of "Freedom" comes up loud, as they cele-brate and dance around, then fades under for:)

CAR. So, it's 8 o'clock in the morning, and I've definitely violated 3 or 4 rules of proper parenting.

LYN. Yeah, kind've ugly at my house too this morning – we had the clothes battle, the eating battle and the did you brush your-hair-brush-your teeth-make your bed-get your homework-don't forget about your snack – what about your lunch – I'll pick you up after school for Brownies frenzy.... *(Music fades out by end of this speech.)*

LEA. What about those Brownie meetings – what's with the silence sign *(holds up hand)* – talk about a cult – the whole thing reeks of a big Kool-Aid Jim Jones kind of moment...

CAR. What gets me is the permission slips – one for the overnight, one to drive to the overnight, and one to sell some overpriced cookies dammit...

LYN. Yeah, well, I got the phone call from the room mother for my son's class – I have to bring in nut-free treats for the class party – so that means I'm swinging by the bakery on my way in...

CAR. Hey at least you're not doing what I did last week – no time because of work so I'm pulling out the Pepperidge Farm and putting the cookies on a plate with a little doily as if nobody's gonna know what I'm doing...

LYN. Please, between the snacks I need to provide for Cub Scouts, bake sales, the Christmas party, the you survived MCAS days, the annual fair, teacher apprecia-tion week, and god knows what else, I feel like Martha Stewart on steroids...

LEA. Oh my god, I'm so glad you said the annual fair, I completely forgot I have to work at that on Saturday afternoon...

CAR. I hate forgetting stuff like that. Like when I just completely forgot to bring my daughter to her best friend's birthday party at Plaster Fun Time. She had been begging me for months to bring her there anyway, and when we got the invitation, I thought, thank god... But then, I just completely forgot about it. Missed the whole thing. And she cried and cried once I realized it. So what did I do? Called her best friend's mother and then hauled the both of them to Plaster Fun Time the next day...

LYN. We all do it though.... I never showed up to volunteer in my kid's class one day. No one came that day to help the poor teacher out...Big L mom *(makes the L sign on her forehead)*.

LEA. I forgot to give my son Valentine's Day cards to bring to school – he was the only one who didn't have them...Yeah, years on the couch for that one...

CAR. Yeah, serious therapy there...it's like what therapists call "unconditional positive regard" for their patients. Like we're supposed to be with our kids. How do I have unconditional positive regard when my kid, you know, picks his nose, then eats it, brings home a friend I hate, loves to fart in public. . . .

LEA. Don't they make you proud? Sometimes I wonder – WHAT HAVE I DONE?

LYN. Well, at least we're past all the screw-ups of when they were babies. It's amazing they are still alive...

CAR. You mean, when my 8-month old rolled down the stairs when I turned my back for 2 seconds? Okay, it was carpeted, there was a landing halfway...But yeah, couldn't shake that off for a while...

LEA. Or when my son used to be colicky and so I read that you should put him on the dryer – and then just barely caught him as the baby seat slid off...

LYN. Yikes…Okay, well back to now, gotta get my run in – I'm the volunteer at the lunch-bunch today at my son's preschool. An hour and a half of watching the little miscreants trying to kill each other and then eat with their mouths open…

CAR. Yeah, well if it makes you feel any better, on Saturday, I have to go to a disco bowling birthday party for 7 year olds.

(LYNETTE and CAROLINE leave LEA onstage.)

LEA. Before I had children, I thought I had it all figured out: my parenting strategy would be one of benign neglect. I figured kids were born with pretty good instincts, and my job would be simply to "guide" them in the right direction. Give them free rein to be who they were born to be, and try not to get too uptight or anxious. And my daughter was born, and she did everything ahead of schedule, and I felt pretty good about all this parenting stuff. And so I went ahead and had another baby, and my son was born. Only this time things were different: my son was born with a hearing loss. Well, I guess you can't really call it a loss, since he never had it to begin with. But within a month of his birth, we knew he would need hearing aids, speech therapy, and special education. Which is certainly not benign. I thought, how is he going to play hockey if he can't hear the coach? Or even get the helmet over the huge honkin' hearing aids? So I became the parent of a "special" child, and dove into a whole new world, one that had me learning a new language and new phrases, like "cochlear implant" and "ear mold." Over the past five years I've been a speech therapist, a parent advocate, an expert on hearing technology. A whole slew of things I never thought of when I got my bachelor's degree in communications – who knew? But, the best part is, he's become a boy. A typical little boy, who runs and plays and talks and sings and tortures his sister. And wears hearing aids. A truly special kid…

(**CAROLINE** *enters, getting off the phone with a babysitter ["Okay – see you Saturday night, right, $12 an hour, we'll see you then…"].*)

CAR. So, my kids are now big enough that I figure it's okay to go out with my husband. Out of the house – alone. Which means finding a babysitter: a person who comes into your home and keeps your children alive in your absence, while you hand over your bank account. The first obstacle is actually IDENTIFYING these people. You can't just ask your neighbor for names; she guards that list like she's Tony Soprano. And you can't just pick up someone else's nanny at the library story time – it's tempting but immoral according to the motherhood code of ethics. So I started by doing surveillance: I'd watch for teenage girls wandering the neighborhood with small children in tow, and strike up a casual conversation. "Oh, you're the BABYSITTER? Are you interested in taking on any other clients?" Then, as time went on I started getting bolder. I was hosting a meeting at my house one night, when one woman asked to use the phone to call her sitter. I pounced. I asked her for her babysitter's number. Score! So that sets me up with my main sitter, and my emergency back-up sitter. But then I wonder, will she feel hurt if I don't call her much? What if one finds out about the other? What if one thinks I'm cheating on her? So I do a careful balancing act, trying to keep each of them busy enough that they'll never suspect I'm actually two-timing them. Of course, this is costing me a small fortune, but it's worth it, if it means I can have a baby-sitter when I need one. Just don't even think to ask me for their numbers… (**CAROLINE** *exits.*)

(**LYNETTE** *enters.*)

LYN. When I was working full-time, taking a vacation day meant scheduling the time with my boss, and dropping the kids at day care. Now that I'm a stay-at-home mom, vacation days are just a dream, or a scheduling nightmare. It means begging every mom I know for the name of a sitter who's available in the middle of a week-day, who won't cause me to re-mortgage my house. It means writing out a list of the routines of each child, down to how my oldest likes her sandwiches and that my youngest will not eat any fruit but pears. And it means begging my husband to be home by 6 o'clock sharp to relieve the sitter.... But last month, I got a mommy vacation day.... I had a colonoscopy. It was a medical necessity, which meant my husband HAD to stay home, so I didn't need to worry about the sitter. Of course, it did entail drinking foul-tasting laxative and lots of time in my bathroom. On the morning of the procedure, I couldn't eat or drink *anything*. I'm starving, uncomfortable, and I'm in an awful hospital gown waiting for medical professionals to do unspeakable things to a part of my body. BUT I'm laying in bed, reading the entire paper without interruption. I'm being covered with warmed-up blankets at regular intervals, and I have a nurse dedicated to me who comes in to make sure I'm as comfortable as possible. They give me glorious drugs to make me sleepy, and afterwards I sleep for as long as I want, until I feel ready to get dressed and go home. I wanted to stay for two days...I know, it's a hell of a way to get a day off. But I need another one next year, and I can hardly wait. *(exits)*

(LYNETTE joins TRICIA, LEA and CAROLINE at the kitchen counter [ad lib hi's].)

CAR. I think it's the fucking laundry that's finally going to put me over the edge...

TRICIA. Yeah, I really think I do something like 17 loads a week...

LEA. Oh, you mean clothes processing? You dump the clothes from the hamper onto your bed so you can put the clothes from the dryer in the hamper, and move the clothes from the washer to the dryer, and take the clothes from the floor and put them in the washer. By the time you fold and put away the clothes on your bed, there's another batch of dirty clothes to start the whole damn process over.

TRICIA. Wow, you actually fold and put the clothes away?

LYN. I think it has to be cleaning.

C&C. Cleaning???

LYN. Yeah, you know, the wiping, sweeping up of crumbs, spills, dirt, gunk; and the picking up of toys, boots, cleats, decomposing Froot Loops...

TRICIA. As soon as you have one part of the house cleaned up, they've gone and trashed up another part, until the only thing you can hope for is that they go to bed...

LYN. Or you just finish sweeping the floor, and they come through trailing dirt. God, I sound like some hausfrau from the fifties – what has happened to my life?

CAR. Wake up and smell the coffee honey, you are a hausfrau from the fifties...

TRICIA. Feed breakfast, make sure everybody gets ready, make the beds, day in, day out, get them and yourself out the door to school, to work...,

LEA. Yeah, thank god for the good moments...

LYN. Sometimes I remember what it's like to be funny and enjoy my kids and it makes the rest of it all right...

TRICIA. Those magic moments that come – not always, but sometimes just when you need them...

CAR. Yeah, like last night when my daughter and I got into a huge laughing fit. Over something so silly, but it was great to share that laugh!

LYN. So sometimes I feel like I got the mom thing worked out okay, but the wife thing on top of that?

TRICIA. So to speak, you mean...

LEA. I assume we're talking about...

CAR. You got it, girlfriend...the whole sex thing...

TRICIA. It's always out there isn't it? The big white elephant in the room...between you and your husband...

LYN. My neighbor has teenagers who are going to be home all summer – so she's worried about *them* having sex in her house, not so much her worry...

LEA. Maybe she should have a "no-sex" policy in the house...

TRICIA. That might not make her husband very happy...

CAR. Really? MY husband would say "What's different? So now you're putting a label on it??"

LYN. Yeah, my husband reads those surveys that say that couples average sex seven times a month, and he wants to know who's getting it that often!

TRICIA. Couples without children??

C&C. Not us!

CAR. And how do you find the time? At the end of the day, I am so damn tired, who has the energy?

LEA. Do it in the morning...

LYN. Get out! Aren't you afraid of the kids walking in??

LEA. No, we get them all set up with breakfast and cartoons, then tell them "mommy has a knot in her back, daddy has to help her work it out", then dead-bolt the door...

TRICIA. At least I don't have to worry about birth control anymore...

CAR. You mean –

TRICIA. Yep, my husband got the big V – snip, snip...I gave birth three times, this was the least he could do.

LYN. Wow, but no more pills, or diaphragms, or condoms – just sex! Like teenagers...Which my husband still thinks like anyway...

CAR. Please, I'm telling my husband about this weird recurring dream, where my teeth keep coming out. They are in pieces and I am freaked in my dream. I ask him what do you think it means? He looks at me and says, "Well, I think it means you should have more sex with your husband."

LEA. It's like the three things you never feel like doing but once you rally, you're glad you did...exercise, church, and sex...

CAR. So now we have a hausfrau and a Stepford wife...

TRICIA. Speaking of church and sex, what about the high holy days of obligation?

LYN. Like your anniversary night.

CAR. Valentine's Day!

TRICIA. Saturday night.

LYN. His birthday.

LEA. Twice a week.

TRICIA. Once a month?

CAR. Vacations.

LYN. New Year's Eve!

CAR. Thanksgiving…

> *(They ad lib off, leaving* **CAROLINE**.*)*

So last Thanksgiving I'm the hostess with the mostest… My neck was in a spasm dealing with all the personality nuances and fighting factions of my extended family. Potatoes to be mashed, gravy boiling, kids needing sledding clothes, my husband wanting shoes off in the house…so anyhow, I'm feeling like Arlo Guthrie here, very Alice's restaurant *(sings)* – *You can get anything you want, at Alice's Restaurant*…and the doorbell's ringing with neighbors who want in on the craziness, I can't get wine in me fast enough because there's too much to do, and my sister-in-law's bitching at me that she can't find the VEGETABLES…big green veggies right in front of her, I point out as I run into the kitchen, smiling but with NASTY wiseass comments going through my head….and then I see my oldest daughter's face, with mashed potatoes all over it, so I grab her, kiss her sweet head and tune out the madness. At which point, she has a loose tooth falling into my hand, fell out right then…So, I finally make it through the rest of the day…I stick some champagne into a snow bank and clean for an hour, neck still throbbing. Then, grab the champagne, and my 3 kids, put George Bailey on the TV, cozy in, and forget the Tooth Fairy. So the next morning my daughter tells me, sardonic already at 8…

the Tooth Fairy blew me off. Shit-fuck-shit-fuck-shit...
SO we talk union rules and holidays even for the Tooth
Fairy, and I thank god it's a whole other year until the
next Thanksgiving. *(She exits, as* **TRICIA** *enters.)*

TRICIA. So my son needed to have some teeth pulled. He
goes to the dentist and is brave and good and the
doctor yanks out two baby teeth after a lot of Novocain
shots and a lot of pulling. That night my son decides
he would put just one tooth under the pillow to make
it easier for the Tooth Fairy. When I checked on him
later, I realize in a panic I don't have anything for him.
I don't like just giving money. Then I remembered the
shelf of emergency goodies. Find something and put it
under the pillow. Kiss him and go to bed. Next morning he comes into my room – "Mom look what the
Tooth Fairy left me – but she forgot to take the tooth!"
Damn. That night, he writes this beautiful little note
to the Tooth Fairy, reminding her about the tooth
and leaves the second one. I FORGET AGAIN about
it until I check on him late at night. Shit. Same panic
for a present. Find one, slip it under his pillow, kiss
him, collapse in my bed. Ohmygawd, forgot to take
the tooth, now TEETH, AGAIN. And, need to write a
note back. Find a tiny piece of paper and a pink glitter
pen. How the hell does the Tooth Fairy write? Write a
note in tiny letters. Take the teeth. Kiss him again. Ah
– motherhood... *(She exits.)*

*(**LEA** and **LYNETTE** are working out at the gym, music
comes up then fades under to while they are talking.)*

LYN. Well, Saturday night when we got home the 13 year
old babysitter was asleep on the floor of the den.

LEA. Hate when that happens.

LYN. I cried the whole time my husband was driving her
home. Nice mother I am, leaving my kids home with a
sleeping 13-year old!

LEA. Yeah, last weekend, we tried calling our babysitter to tell her we were going to a different place and to give her the number, and she didn't answer for 2 HOURS. When we finally got home and asked her what the hell she was doing – she said – "just don't tell my dad I was on the phone with my boyfriend, okay?"

LYN. Well, it's just been a banner week for me anyway...you know, where there was something going on *every* day after school. I swore I wouldn't let that happen, and yet here it is – Brownies, soccer practice, piano lessons, aaagh....

LEA. It starts as soon as they get off the bus...mayhem... Backpacks flying, papers strewn, struggle to get home-work started, CCD, the afternoon shuttling.

LYN. I've mastered the art of multitasking while driving – it's gotten so I can help one kid with their homework, throw soccer clothes to another one to change into, pass back some form of dinner/snack, and listen to my youngest go on about her day, all while careening around town in the minivan...

LEA. Yeah, I've helped my kids with homework in the car, waiting at the dentist office, in the morning over breakfast, you name it...

LYN. Who knew that all the schooling we went through would actually come in handy at this point...

LEA. Now if only I could remember any of it...

(They exit, as the music fades out.)

(CAR enters.)

CAR. Can we talk about homework for a minute? I really don't mean to complain but after 10 years of cooking, cleaning, diapers, sleep deprivation, emotional nur-turing and juggling the lives of my entire family I'm supposed to be a fucking math tutor as well? I mean... do you remember how to measure the area of a rectangle? I'm sorry, when have I ever used this infor-mation in my life? Or solve this one...you have a bag of tulip bulbs...10 white ones, 3 red ones, and 3 pink ones, and 6 have been randomly removed. How many tulip bulbs do you need to plant to guarantee getting a white tulip? Are you kidding me?? Why wouldn't I just buy white tulip bulbs if I want white tulips? Or express 333 thousandths as a decimal...ok, that's easy...it's either .00333 or .333? So these problems are coming home, and my anxiety is rising. I'm hanging in there, but I can see that my daughter is figuring out that I am not exactly whipping the answers off the top of my head. And I just hate that look in her eyes, "mommy doesn't know everything?" Shit she is only 9, this is way too soon for her to figure out that she is probably smarter than I am. So, I'm trying to act like I am in TOTAL control. Yesterday, I'm reading ahead of her in the math work sheet – my latest trick to buy time – and I told her I had to go to the bathroom. I grabbed my cell phone, ran into the bathroom, called my friend at work and asked her to do a quick review of decimals for me. Thank God, I understood...I'm so afraid. What the hell am I going to do when she hits 5th grade math? *(exits)*

(**LEA** *enters.*)

LEA. I've always thought if had I lived in the old days, that I would be this sort've Ma Ingalls type – you know Little House on the Prairie – capable, gentle, brave, able to churn butter and make all our clothes and take care of the farm animals...And yet, we have come to depend on all the comfort and convenience that is life in the modern age – and nowhere is this more evident than at the supermarket. So I'm standing there one day, in the checkout line, and as I load the weekly $200 worth of groceries onto the conveyor belt – I'm thinking – good god, everything my kids eat comes out of a BOX. Cereal, cookies to eat, cookies to make, cake mix, breakfast bars, fruit snacks, crackers, goldfish, mac and cheese, mashed potatoes, MASHED POTATOES, frozen dinners, frozen waffles, frozen French toast, frozen pancakes, frozen hamburgers – my face is frozen just looking at the stuff. You talk about *conspicuous consumption* – I am staring down at what is coming out my cart, and it's like – look, finally – something from the produce aisle! A banana – direct from the tree! Real apples! Okay, so like $12 worth is in its natural state – pretty much direct from nature and not mutated into some other form – and the rest of it is boxed food. Like I'm some sort of militia mom stocking up for the overthrow of the government...So, not Ma Ingalls...Not even close... *(exits)*

(LYNETTE, CAROLINE and TRICIA enter– CAROLINE carries in shots and glasses of adult beverages. Restaurant music comes up for set change and fades under for beginning of dialogue.)

CAR. Thank god I made it out of the house. What a day...

TRICIA. I know, I just looked at my husband finally and said – sorry but I am OUTA here...

(All down their shots – then toast with their glasses.)

LYN. I don't know how you do it, working full time...

TRICIA. In some ways it's really hard because you feel like you are never doing any one of your jobs all the way – your day job or your mom job. In other ways it's easier because things are compartmentalized – I'm at work now and I do work things – and I can get other stuff done too because I don't have the kids on me all day...

CAR. I know, trying to work part-time out of the house is a bitch sometimes...I careen back and forth between laundry and an important phone call...try and type an e-mail while the kids are in the room shouting they're hungry...Some days I just long to be in an office and FOCUS...

LYN. All I know is that I had one of THOSE days.... The sort of "beat the clock" thing from the moment you open your eyes and the day starts...Off to the races, let's go...As I was making lunch for the three kids, shouting instructions about getting ready, letting the dog out, writing a note for school and blow drying my hair – simultaneously, I suddenly got the kids' song in my head from Barney or somewhere years ago... Hurry, hurry drive the fire truck, hurry, hurry, drive the fire truck...

CAR. Hurry, hurry, drive the fire truck...

TRICIA. Ding, ding, ding, ding, ding...

LYN. Yeah, that's it! And instead I'm thinking, hurry, hurry, make the lunches...

TRICIA. Hurry, hurry, start commuting...

CAR. Hurry, hurry, dump the groceries...

ALL. Ding, ding, ding, ding, ding

(They get faster and faster as they sing...)

CAR. Hurry, hurry do some laundry...

TRICIA. Hurry, hurry, write some e-mails...

LYN. Hurry, hurry, make some phone calls...

ALL. Ding, ding, ding, ding, ding...

CAR. Hurry, hurry, pick up children...

TRICIA. Hurry, hurry curse the traffic...

LYN. Hurry, hurry, help with homework...

ALL. Ding, ding, ding, ding, ding ..

(All inhale, and then...)

CAR. Hurry, hurry, nurture children...

TRICIA. Hurry, hurry, drive to soccer...

LYN. Hurry, hurry, wish for valium...

ALL. Ding, ding, ding, ding, ding

(All take big breath and then...)

CAR. Hurry, hurry, love your children

TRICIA. Hurry, hurry, love your husband

LYN. Hurry, hurry, love the hamster

ALL. Ding, ding, ding, ding, ding

CAR. Hurry, hurry, feed them dinner,

TRICIA. Hurry, hurry, tuck the kids in,

LYN. Hurry, hurry, yell your head off...

ALL. Ding, ding, ding, ding, ding

   (All take a big breath, then....)

CAR. Hurry, hurry, bang some wine back

TRICIA. Hurry, hurry, fake the orgasm

LYN. Hurry, hurry, take the Prozac...

ALL. DING, DING, DING, DING, DING!

   (All toast with glasses, then they exit. **LEA** *enters.)*

LEA. I don't care what anyone says. It does get easier as they get older. Yeah I know, little kids, little problems, big kids, big problems...But still, I think there's a sort've honeymoon phase when they are not so tiny and dependent and vulnerable and yet they're not fresh and hormonal and dangerous behind the wheel. And that's what I'm enjoying now. That middle stage. It's like the middle trimester of pregnancy – when you feel great – and you are mostly over your morning sickness and you have the glow and you're not desperate for it all to be over. So between the ages of say, 6 and 12, as far as I can tell, it's the "golden years" of parenthood, and I for one am enjoying it!

   (She stays onstage, as **TRICIA** *enters.)*

TRICIA. I wonder every day if I'm doing the right thing. Should I quit work? Lose the career? Make do without the paycheck? Am I missing out on crucial mommy moments? But then I get to work and I'm glad, and I think, happy mom, happy kids. And we get through the day and the week as a family, and it mostly manages to work out. So I guess I'll just keep on going, unless, until, well, just keep on going.... *(stays onstage)*

   *(***LYNETTE** *enters.)*

LYN. There are times when I look at my daughter – all of 7 and not weighing more than 43 pounds soaking wet, and I think, she looks so tiny...so young...she's still just my little, little girl...and then there are those times, like when she got all dressed up the other day, big girl velour shirt, skirt, tights, good church shoes with a bit of a heel, and I thought, my god, she looks 16 years old...Like she's ready to go on her first date, absolutely gorgeous, with a killer smile and standing so tall and poised...And I just get overwhelmed with it all...How can it be? My sweet little girl – is she all grown up? Have I done a good job with her so far? Is it too late if I haven't? They say everything you can give a child matters until about age 8 and after that it's – the ship has sailed, the bus has left the station, good luck to you and hope for the best...I really hope that's not true – it can't be true...This little thing has so much to learn still, so much happiness to live, so many hurts to get through...But then I look at her again and think she's lived so much hurt and happiness already...

CAR. Late at night, after I've picked up the Legos, and sorted the trucks and animals into their designated bins, after I've put the homework in the backpacks and set the lunch boxes on the counter for the next day, I creep into their bedrooms to stare at their sleeping selves. Neurotic that I am, I do check, even now, to see that they're breathing, but I also study their faces, relaxed in sleep, looking so different from their daytime selves. And this I know: that when I look back at my life from the other end, this will be the happy time, the time I miss most, that interval between toddler and teenager, when they can dress and feed and care for themselves but still require three hugs and two kisses before letting me leave them to their dreams. And I try to savor that feeling, storing it inside my heart for later, as I stumble to bed.

(10,000 Maniacs's "These Are the Days" fades up fast and loud as she finishes talking, and lights go to black.)

End Act I

---

*Please see Music Use Note on Page 3.

ACT 2

(All four enter as Bowie's "Under Pressure" plays. The song fades out as* **LYN** *talks.)*

LYN. I don't know why the corporate world is so conde-scending about refusing to give mothers credit for time served at home. Because after I had children, I realized just how relevant motherhood is to corporate life. Hey, who's better at multi-tasking than a mother? If she can chop vegetables while making a doctor's appointment for her toddler while reviewing her first grader's artwork, don't you think she can handle a middle management job? After all, how hard can it be to manage a group of direct reports when you've dealt with sibling rivalry? Convince an employee to take on a detestable assignment when you've convinced your 2-year-old to pee in the toilet? Stare down an opposi-tional co-worker during a crucial meeting when you've given "the look" to your 8-year-old, the one that causes him to confess to locking his younger brother in the closet? I think Corporate America should hire **MORE** stay-at-home moms: maybe then they'd see productiv-ity rise, and more clean hands and noses. I think it's a corporate conspiracy…

TRICIA. When is it that you really become "mom?" You know, Mom in the sense that your mother is "Mom." When my daughter was just a brand new baby, it was Christmas and I wanted to inscribe a book I bought for her. I couldn't sign it "love, Mommy" because I didn't feel like "Mommy." She wasn't talking, so she wasn't calling me anything. She was a little gurgling bundle – and I was just barely adjusting to the fact that

* Please see Music Use Note on page 3.

I was a PARENT of anything…So, I inscribed the book – "love, Mom" which seemed ridiculous too. Mom was my mom, my mother, the woman who had raised four children…. So my little girl begins to talk – you know Ma Ma, Da Da and she graduates to Mommy in that tiny little 2-year old voice and before long she's screaming MOMMMY at me when she's four and then she's a second grader and now I'm occasionally Mom. But it still doesn't hit me that I am Mom the way my mom is MOM, if you know what I mean. And then one day, she's talking to her cousin, and her cousin says something about "well, your mom said we should…" And it hits me. Ohmygawd. I am now "MOM" – you know – all capital letters. As in "I have to ask my mom." Or, "My mom won't let me." "My mom drives me crazy." Or worse to come, "I hate my mother"… Like all the rest of it, it's a funny, scary part of motherhood… *(She exits.)*

LEA. I don't know why they call it the "terrible twos…" My son is five, and he's still in the throes of it. We battle over short sleeves in winter, the necessity of socks with shoes, you name it. Anyway, one morning he asks if I'll pick him up after school, instead of taking the bus home, and I'm feeling good, no fights about socks that day, so I say yes. And he is so happy, reminds me to write a note to his teacher and call the bus company. And I pick him up, and he is so excited, and we have a lovely afternoon. Then we get to bath time, always a frightening time in our house. He hates to stop what he's doing to get in the tub, so I have to practically drag him kicking and screaming; then once he's in, he won't come out. And because he can't wear hearing aids in the tub, I'm screaming at him to "KEEP THE WATER IN THE TUB!" and he's turning away so he can't read my lips, and by the time bath time is over we are BOTH soaked and angry and at least one of us is in tears…Usually me…I battle him into his jammies, stick his hearing aids back into his ears, and he angrily puts himself in bed; then I lay down next to him for our ritual snuggle. And I turn to him and say "so what was your favorite part of today?" and he turns his tearstained face to me and says "when you picked me up from school." And my heart just melts...

(**LYNETTE** *and* **CAROLINE** *at the coffee shop again*)

CAR. So, what wore me down yesterday, no – forget that, every day, is the discipline thing...

LYN. I know, it's like you just spend the whole day saying no, and trying not to give in to negotiating every little thing...

CAR. It's all about manipulation anyway. What they do to us, what we do to them. My favorite discipline trick is when I threaten to take something away that I don't want them to have anyway. Talk about a win-win.

LYN. How about when it happens the other way though... you know...that sucks...

CAR. Yeah, when you're mad and you say – that's it – no computer games for 2 days – and then it's like, shit! Why did I do that?

LYN. It's better when you take something away that you weren't going to do anyway...Now we are not going to go to the movies!

CAR. Yeah, we WERE going to go to the movies, but TOO BAD, now we're not...

LYN. The things you find yourself doing sometimes...

CAR. My moral authority can be so depleted as a parent... My son was being so bad the other day, and nothing was working. Talk about desperate – I finally invoked the 10 Commandments – you know Honor thy father and mother...

LYN. Well, whatever it takes!

CAR. It's all about who is doing the manipulating...

LYN. Yeah, one time we were at Wal Mart, and I was trying to get through the check out and get out of there, and my son takes off, and I chase him down and drag him back to check out, and he's screaming "you are not my mommy!"

CAR. Wow…That is so conniving!

LYN. I know! Hey, what's with all these awful "parties" we get sucked into?

CAR. Talk about your desperate housewives. Southern Living? Pampered Chef? Or is it Southern Chef and Pampered Living….I don't know…

LYN. Nasty Nighties, Bath & Body Works, Mary Kay, Tupperware, Longaberger Baskets….the list goes on.

CAR. And nobody wants to go, except for the night out and a guaranteed glass of wine….

LYN. What about the scrap booking thing? My sister-in-law just went with her girlfriends for a whole scrap booking weekend! She had a blast.

CAR. What about the dreaded Southern Living Party gone awry? 2 a.m., drunkenly ordering god knows what sort of crap. Confederate flag cheese slicer, anyone?

LYN. Is there a party that offers how to books for parents – like how to have the big sex talk with your fourth grader?

CAR. If there is, I don't want to go, I'm going to take a yoga class instead.…

*(Yoga music starts as **CAROLINE** gets her yoga mat and blanket. Lights dim. She sets up in meditation pose. Music fades under while she is talking.)*

CAR. "Ahh…shivasana…final relaxation…time to let go of the practice into conscious meditation…Breathe in….breathe out…relaxxx…Shhhiit, Valentine's Day is tomorrow. Gotta buy cards for all the kids to give to their classmates. Then help them sign and address 20 each. I fucking hate Valentine's Day. It is so unbelievably fake…breathe in…breathe out…belly rises…belly falls…I love how sensual I feel at the end of my practice. I love this peace. I wish my husband was lying next to me. I always think so sensually of him when I am at yoga…Why does it fade the minute he walks in the door?…breathe in….breathe out…belly rises….belly falls…..Maybe I'll have sex with him for

Valentine's Day?...Breathe in....breathe out...Maybe not......belly rises....belly falls....... God, my son is so wired.......every morning he wakes up complaining about his day.... "Is it a school day today mommy? I hate school." Breathe in.......breathe out...He can be such a little asshole.....belly rises....belly falls............ thoughts drift away like clouds...The woman next to me is snoring. That is so distracting. Breathe in, breathe out...I am so going to Dunkin Donuts after this. *(performs prayer ritual for final namaste)* Ashanti – Ashanti – Peace."

(Yoga music fades up briefly and out as **TRICIA** *enters.)*

TRICIA. I can't believe it, but my nine year old daughter is starting to ask "those" questions. Already. I didn't have a clue about sex until I was....I don't know......20? Anyhow, I'm determined to have her understand, be comfortable, feel good about all of it. You know, no hang-ups, keep it real, respect herself, all that...So I find this awesome book and we decide that Sunday nights she'll read a chapter, and we'll talk about it together afterwards. After my other kids are asleep... So the first "talk" is easy...differences between men and women. How girls develop. And when. No biggie...Then a couple of Sundays later, she's finished the book. Which means the whole intercourse thing has been covered. Okay, here we go to tonight's talk ....Big deep breath, fire in the fireplace, just the two of us....a Little House on the Prairie moment. So she says, "Mom? Can I ask a couple of questions?" "Anything," I say. "Okay, I get how men have sperm and girls have eggs. But how do the sperm get to the eggs? Are they magnetic or something?" Shit. I guess she didn't really get the whole intercourse chapter too well. "Ahh, no... they're not magnetic, they sort of jump from the end of the man's penis into the woman. And then they go and find the egg." "How do they know where to go?" she asks. "Well the man's body and the woman's body kind of line up perfectly. Like puzzle pieces."

Puzzle pieces? God she'll need a shrink for sure…
"Puzzle pieces?" she asks. "Yes, they fit together and
it feels nice and then the sperm can find the eggs."
What the hell am I doing? "But how does the sperm
know it wants to?" she asks. "Ahh, it's like instinct."
"Instinct?" she asks. "What's that?" "Well, instinct. Let's
see….Like when you wake up in the morning and you
smell bacon. And pancakes. And your instinct says…
I'm hungry." "Oh. Okay. Yeah, I like pancakes and
bacon. Okay." There's intercourse. Puzzle pieces and
pork products. Jesus.

(She exits as **LEA** *enters.)*

LEA. Every week I take my kids to the YMCA for swimming
lessons. After class we ALWAYS stop in the lounge for
a snack from the vending machine. My daughter reli-
giously chooses Cinnamon Sugar Pop Tarts and my
son usually gets Nacho Cheese Doritos. There is always
one mom waiting in the lounge, while her son takes
his lesson. She seems pretty cool. She's tall and thin
and I've seen her snacking on Balance Bars and carrots. So, we are there, getting our weekly snacks and
she is there too, this time with her 5 year old daughter. Who is watching us make our vending machine
selections. The girl turns to her mom and says "Mom,
I want a snack." The mother pulls out carrots from
her bag. "No," the girl insists, "I want something from
here" pointing to the vending machine. "No Honey,"
says the mom. "I want THOSE chips," the girl says,
pointing to the Doritos my son is munching on. "NO."
"Why not?" "Because." Because why?" "BECAUSE."
Now I am DYING to finish her thought…. "Because
it's JUNK FOOD and we DON'T EAT that." And I'm
sort of enjoying the fact that she is so uncomfortable, unable to articulate any other reason besides
BECAUSE. Because it's so obvious what she would say
if we weren't there. And suddenly, I am flying down
memory lane, remembering the years I grew up with a
Mom who didn't let my sisters and me eat junk food.

I'm talking about a woman who gave us saltines for treats. Who parceled out our Halloween candy. Who did not buy soft, white bread. Oh my god, I was insane for junk food. In 4th grade, I traded my entire lunch for Ring Dings. I chose friends based on the snack food they had. And I finally even learned to hide my Halloween candy before I went in for the night. SO I'm feeling real sympathy for the child, empathy for the mom and even for myself. What's the right path? What is good eating? Is there BAD food? As I gather the troops, I silently acknowledge us...Moms.... always walking the tightrope when it comes to all the manifestations of care, nutrition, health...love.

(**LEA** *joins* **TRICIA**, **CAROLINE**, *and* **LYNETTE** *at the bar.*)

CAR. Okay: question...would you rather have a birthday party for your seven year old or a root canal...with light sedation.

LYN. I'd go for the birthday party, but not by much. I do love that light sedation.

TRICIA. Yeah, the cute invites, do you have to ask the whole class, what about the kid who rips the heads off the Barbies? Is he in? And does his mother get to come and spend an hour droning on about how friggin GIFTED he is? Ya, gifted. Got a real knack for dismembering.

LEA. And do you have it at your house, and wind up scraping Spiderman frosting off your dining room rug....

LYN. Or pay a million dollars to have it at some paintball rip-off place? The bathroom trips, the whining, the injuries.....

CAR. What about the goody bags? Who the hell started this? I mean whose birthday is it anyway?

TRICIA. And what's in them but $15 worth of crap...stickers, gum, candy that will rip your kids teeth out..

LYN. In fact....why doesn't the *mother* get the party on the children's birthdays....I mean all the baby did was show up.

LEA. Exactly…

TRICIA. I gotta ask you guys something…Do you guys sort of rate the gifts you get?

LYN. Rate?

TRICIA. Okay, my daughter went to a party for one of her very best friends. We got a cute outfit at the Gap, made the wrapping paper, decorated it with stickers and pipe cleaners, taped candy to the top….the whole deal..

CAR. Okay, Martha…

TRICIA. Well this was a good friend! So anyhow, I hate to say this, but my daughter's party comes two weeks later, and this same girl…

LYN. Gap girl?

TRICIA. Yeah, Gap girl…well she comes with a box of sidewalk chalk for her gift. That's a $2.50 gift tops…

CAR. Did you rip the Gap clothes off her?

TRICIA. No…But I thought about it…

LEA. Alright, since we're doing true confessions here…anybody recycle a gift?

TRICIA. Please!

CAR. All the time.

LEA. Last Saturday I totally spaced on a birthday party for a kid from my daughter's dance class. Had no time to go buy anything.

TRICIA. What'd you do?

LEA. Yanked something right out of the closet that hadn't been used yet, taped a card on it and we're good to go….

LYN. I keep a bunch of crappy gifts my kids have gotten that I hate…you know, make your own slushies…

CAR. Colored sand ornament makers…

TRICIA. Books with 365 craft ideas for mom…

ALL. AAAGGHH…

LEA. Yup. All that stuff. Anyhoo, in the post-party frenzy, I separate out all the stuff I can't deal with, and put them in my closet. Then, in a pinch….

LYN. You'd better be careful! I did that and gave back the present to the same kid who gave it! Luckily, I ranted on about how much we loved the one she gave to us, how we wanted to get one for her.....

CAR. Liar, liar pants on fire!

LYN. Hey, whatever it takes.

CAR. Remind me not to chintz out on your kids' birthday...

TRICIA. I can't remind you about anything – I have no brain myself...

LEA. What's turning my brain to mush is the things I say over and over again, every single day...

LYN. It's like, all I do is nag, nag, nag, like push the tape recorder to play and repeat...

TRICIA. Look both ways!

CAR. Take your plate to the sink, please

LYN. One thing at a time...

LEA. What do you mean, there's nothing to do...

CAR. Don't tell me you're bored...

TRICIA. Read a book. Go outside.

LYN. Did someone step on a cat or are you whining?

CAR. CAN YOU TURN THAT DOWN PLEASE

LEA. Don't forget your coat!

TRICIA. Don't forget your hat!

CAR. Your mittens!

LYN. Your homework!

LEA. Your snack!

TRICIA. Your saxophone!

LYN. I told you to go before we left the house.

CAR. Can you hold it?

LEA. You'll have to hold it.

TRICIA. See what happens when you don't listen to me?

LEA. Mommy is right about a lot of things...

CAR. And I really do love you, even when I'm angry...

LYN. I always love you, no matter what...

TRICIA. You are doing great, I am so proud of you!

LEA. That's terrific!

CAR. Way to go, honey!

LYN. You are my best boy!

TRICIA. My best girl!

CAR. Make your bed, please.

LYN. Brush your teeth.

LEA. Have you brushed your teeth?

TRICIA. I asked you to brush your teeth.

LYN. Fine. Don't brush them. Let your teeth fall out.

LEA. If it's itchy, you're not wiping it right.

CAR. 3 wipes per flush!

LYN. Stop fighting with your brother.

CAR. I'm not going to ask you again.

TRICIA. This is all going to end with someone getting hurt!

CAR. *(to offstage)* No whipping with rubber snakes!

LEA. Don't tell me it's not your turn…

CAR. It isn't always equal but it's always fair.

LYN. It's not a democracy here.

TRICIA. *(to offstage)* Stop yelling, if you want to ask me something, come here!

CAR. *(yelling)* DON'T YOU YELL AT ME LIKE THAT!

LEA. Keep your hand out of your pants, please.

TRICIA. Yes, sometimes it's big and sometimes it's small.

CAR. You'll need to talk to your father about that.

TRICIA. It's not evacuation…it's ejaculation.

LYN. Turn off the TV.

CAR. Turn off the play station.

TRICIA. Turn off the computer.

CAR. Are you going to make me come in there and turn that off myself?

LYN. You can think it, but don't you dare say it.

LEA. I don't want to hear another word out of you...

TRICIA. If I have to say it ONE MORE TIME...

LEA. Uh, uh, uh...not another word – uh, uh, uh!

CAR. LET'S GO!

LEA. Is your seat belt buckled?

LYN. Remember: smile even if you hate the present, okay?

CAR. I hate to say I told you so...

LEA. Just because everyone else does it, doesn't mean we do it...

TRICIA. You'll thank me some day...

CAR. It's a good thing you're good looking, or I'd have to sell you for a dollar.

(They leave, except for **TRICIA.***)*

TRICIA. I fell in love again with my daughter. Lots of eye contact, cuddling, and discovery. Rapture. Tuning the world out, complete in each other. The sort of weekend you don't want to end, because you know these don't happen often. And it's like a gift, at 42, to have this feeling again. It happened in a hospital room. She was sick, we went to the hospital. Blinking machines, tubes, and shitty food. My other kids stayed home, my husband too. So it was just us, alone for the first time since she was born. And I looked at her like Dorothy looks at Aunt Em after her trip to Munchkinland. Like I've never seen her, or I *have* seen her but didn't fully appreciate her. My baby, my youngest. Little forehead. Perfect eyebrows. One dimple. Why haven't I seen her? Really seen her? I know why, really, it's a function of time. The third child, the third breakfast to get, third kid to do everything.... But God, she's beautiful. I'm like a dying woman, greedy, smelling her in, and lying next to her, holding her hand and staring at her when she sleeps. Three days of Candyland and comfort and us. And only her to love. But when we come home, we both feel it – the spell is broken. Others want us and need us. But we try to steal away, we sneak to her room, and I read to her alone in her bed, until my other kids come too, wanting me that way. Deserving me that way. So I'll try to steal the moments. Like Dorothy, I've seen the light. Had my own little trip to the Emerald City. And got the chance to strip everything away for a little bit and relish one of my three gifts.

LEA. My youngest son is 5 – he's going to be going to kindergarten. And I'm getting old. Peeking at Botox flyers, no clue who Beyonce *(or latest pop singer)* is. You know, one day you're ass deep in sick kids on February vacation, crusty noses, sore bums, vomit. You don't read anything anymore, you love till you're limp, and you dream of what it will be like to not be so needed, so yanked on, so critical to everyone else's survival. And then there you are, somehow you're there. You've made it! You've plowed through the small kid phase, no time, really, to reflect on it while it's happening. Coupla cursory video clips of the key things, you know, Christmas, birthdays, summer vacation. And then the last child goes to school. And you gotta figure out your own day. Pantyhose and a job? Casseroles and Oprah? Something in between? It's like that recurring dream I have where I show up to a class I've never attended, and the professor is handing out the final exam. I don't have a clue! About the economics test or about who I want to be now. I will, of course, always be a mother. Friend, wife, daughter, sister. But what about me? It's test time, and I've gotta come up with the essay. *(stays onstage)*

LYN. I never thought I'd make it through those first years as a mom. Actually, I just barely survived on a lot of levels…. It's so much easier now in some ways but the truth is, there's hard stuff at every age, isn't there? True, when they're babies you don't get the rolling eyes, the hurtful blow-offs, the sassing back. But you don't get any sleep either. And not a ton of doing anything outside of the house that isn't a big car-seat-binkies-pack-the-wipes-diapers-bottles-formula-goldfish-in-a-bag-extra-outfit in case there's another up-the-back-poop event. Getting to Stop & Shop is like planning the invasion of Normandy. Okay, so the lesson is, mothering is hard all the time. I get it. But I've got to say, the older stuff *is* scarier. Because it's as if you take that beautiful baby you've come to know better than anyone ever will and throw her out to the world. Roll the dice with her, go for the big jackpot.... take a chance! And all the mother control you've come to resent looks like a wonderful haven. Now the rest of the world can wield control and it can all go wrong. What if she meets the guy with the cold eyes at the Harvard Square T-station, thinks he's intriguing, cool...someone she can help...Then he stomps out the glint in her eye...with comments, head games, the weight of his own falling star. Then what? Maybe she'll recover, maybe she'll grow stronger and smarter from the experiences, better about herself. Good, even. But I'll tell you what: if someone offered me a pass on the big friggin roulette game, I'd take it in a minute. But like every other mother, I've gotta play this round.

CAR. Before I had kids I always felt like I was a fun and funny person. Sarcasm and irony were my favorite forms of expression. Then I became a mom – a worried, neurotic bundle of nerves – with each child just exacerbating the humorless condition of my over-thinking. The kids were funny and cute, and I ate up all they offered, but me, not so funny...or cute. Too busy getting through the day with any semblance of sanity and parental judgment intact. But here's the best part. My kids are growing up. Growing older. Developing their own wonderful personalities. Getting irony, loving sarcasm. And I'm getting mine back too. And now we are enjoying laughs together. Our own little family repartee going back and forth. Inside jokes. Shared laughter. Amazing. All of it. I can't wait for more.

(Emotions "You've Got the Best of My Love" fades up loud as the lights dim and stays on through the curtain call.*)

End Act 2

---

* Please see Music Use Note on Page 3.

SET DESCRIPTION

Upstage center – Four 4 x 8 flats sponge-painted in grey and blue forming one wall. In front of that wall was a set of four open faced lockers, painted in a dark blue with pink trim, where each character placed their props.

Stage right: Three panel black and white folding screen, with two wood theater chairs in front, also painted in same color scheme as the flats.

Stage left: We built a rotating set piece that looked like a kitchen counter on one side, a bar on the other (had a foot rail like a bar) and the front end had a velcroed piece that, when removed, made it look like two characters were sitting at a Starbuck's-like restaurant. We used three stools that could pass in a kitchen or a bar – two on the SR side, one of the SL side.

Note: *Each character had a color theme that was pulled through costumes and props. For instance, Tricia's color was purple, so she had a purplish bag/briefcase for the parenting books, a backpack with purple in it hung in her locker with her props, her costumes were in that color family, etc. It helped to cement the identity of each character, if only in a subtle way.*

SET DRESSING

4 Backpacks
4 kid umbrellas
Sports equipment: soccer ball, rollerblades, baseball glove and bat
Notebooks/binders/books

Kid jackets

PROPERTY LIST

ACT I

Prescription bottle
2 Starbucks cups
4 Coffee mugs
Bag/briefcase with parenting books
Cell phone
Dynaband
2 Small hand weights/dumbbells
4 Shot glasses
4 Wine glasses
Wooden tray (for carrying glasses into scene)

ACT II

4 Coffee mugs
Yoga mat

COSTUME PLOT

ACT I

CAROLYN:
Neutral pants (gray, tan, etc.), casual tops, walking shoes

TRICIA:
Working mom clothes
Accessories for scene with wine: scarves, necklaces, jacket

LYNETTE:
Black workout pants, casual top, hooded sweatshirt, sneakers

LEA:
Workout pants, casual top, sneakers

ACT II

CAROLYN:
Yoga pants, casual top (for working out)

TRICIA:
Working mom clothes – (different top than Act I)

LEA:
Neutral pants, casual top (different from Act I)

LYNETTE:
Jeans, casual top, walking shoes

OTHER TITLES AVAILABLE FROM SAMUEL FRENCH

THE MOMologues

Lisa Rafferty, Stefanie Cloutier, and Sheila Eppolito

Comedy / 4f / Simple Set

This original comedy about motherhood rips away the gauzy mask of parenthood to reveal what all mothers know but don't always talk about: it's overwhelming and exhausting, but also very, very funny. From the joys of infertility, through reading the same books over and over and over, to finally seeing your baby get on that school bus, this play mines the laughs and tears of the early years of motherhood. Four separate characters tell their individual stories, either directly to the audience in monologues, or in scenes with each other. Mothers everywhere can relate to the labor stories, the frustration of a simple trip to the store, the quest to connect with other mothers, all of which causes them to plan moms' nights out and arrive in packs to laugh hysterically at this tribute to "the toughest job you'll ever love.

"The show is about the ups and downs of motherhood; what binds mothers together, not what sets them apart...edgy, funny, and true."
– *Showcase Magazine*

"At the show we caught Saturday, the audience frequently exploded in laughter."
– *The Boston Globe*

"Reveals the funny, secretive side of having kids!"
– *Parents & Kids Magazine*

OTHER TITLES AVAILABLE FROM SAMUEL FRENCH

FUNNY, YOU DON'T LOOK LIKE A GRANDMOTHER

Book and Lyrics by Lois Wyse and Sheilah Rae
Music by Robert Waldman

Musical Comedy Revue / 4 or 5f, 2m / Unit prop set / 1 or 2 pianos + optional band

Funny, You Don't Look Like a Grandmother is a humorous, heartwarming revue that looks at modern grandmothers in a whole new light. These are the women who have thrown away the granny glasses, shapeless black dresses and Red Cross shoes and replaced them with cute little tennis dresses, skis and a condo in Florida. The show celebrates these changes with skits and songs about everything from what to name the grandmother to her availability as baby sitter, her job, her friends, her activities, her new interest in shopping, but most of all, her relationship to that incredible new baby and its parents. Whether you are a grandparent or a grandchild, every generation of your family will love this show!

"It could be another *Nunsense* or *Forever Plaid* — Check it out!"
– Price Berkley, Publisher, Theatrical Index

"Funny! This musical revue looks like a winner...laughs for the whole family."
– The Los Angeles Times

"*Grandmother* mixes clever, tuneful songs, a sparklingly witty book, and recognizable characters to serve up a pleasant treat."
– Miami Herald